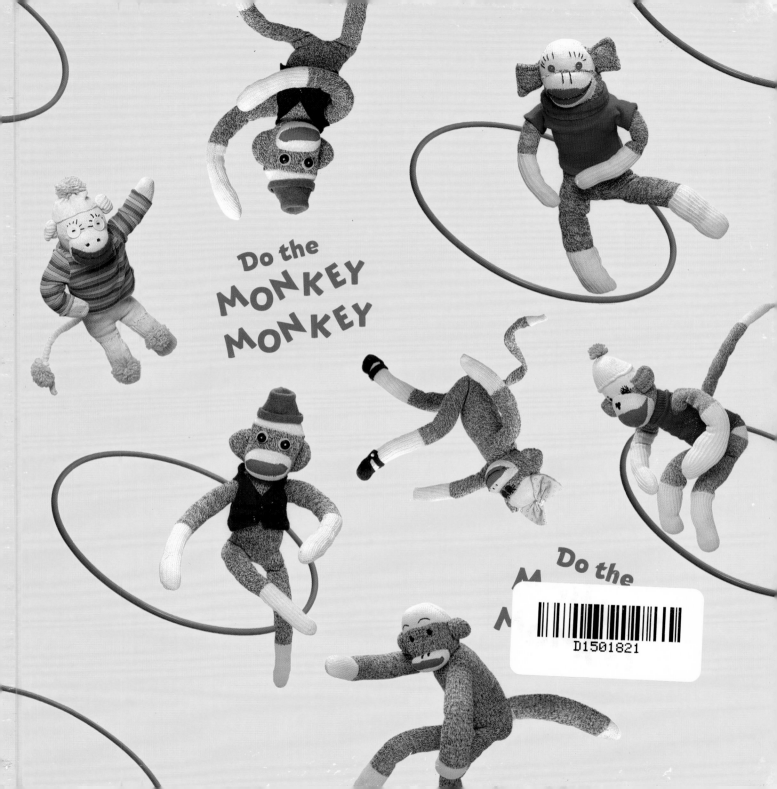

Do the
MONKEY
MONKEY

Do the
M
M

D1501821

Library of Congress Cataloging-in-Publication Data Available

2   4   6   8   10   9   7   5   3   1

Published by Sterling Publishing Co., Inc.
387 Park Avenue South, New York, NY 10016
Text copyright © 2005 by Harriet Ziefert Inc.
Photographs copyright © 2005 by William B. Winburn
Distributed in Canada by Sterling Publishing
c/o Canadian Manda Group, 165 Dufferin Street
Toronto, Ontario, Canada M6K 3H6
Distributed in Great Britain and Europe by Chris Lloyd at Orca Book
Services, Stanley House, Fleets Lane, Poole BH15 3AJ, England
Distributed in Australia by Capricorn Link (Australia) Pty. Ltd.
P.O. Box 704, Windsor, NSW 2756, Australia

Printed in China

Sterling ISBN 1-4027-2849-2

Sock Monkeys

Do the
MONKEY
MONKEY!

Photos by William B. Winburn

Sterling Publishing Co., Inc.
New York

You stick your
RIGHT PAW
IN.

You stick your
RIGHT PAW
OUT.

You do the MONKEY MONKEY
and you swing yourself around.

That's how
we dance and shout!

You stick your
LEFT PAW
IN.

You stick your
LEFT PAW
OUT.

You do the MONKEY MONKEY
and you swing yourself around.

That's how
we dance and shout!

You stick your
RIGHT FOOT
IN.

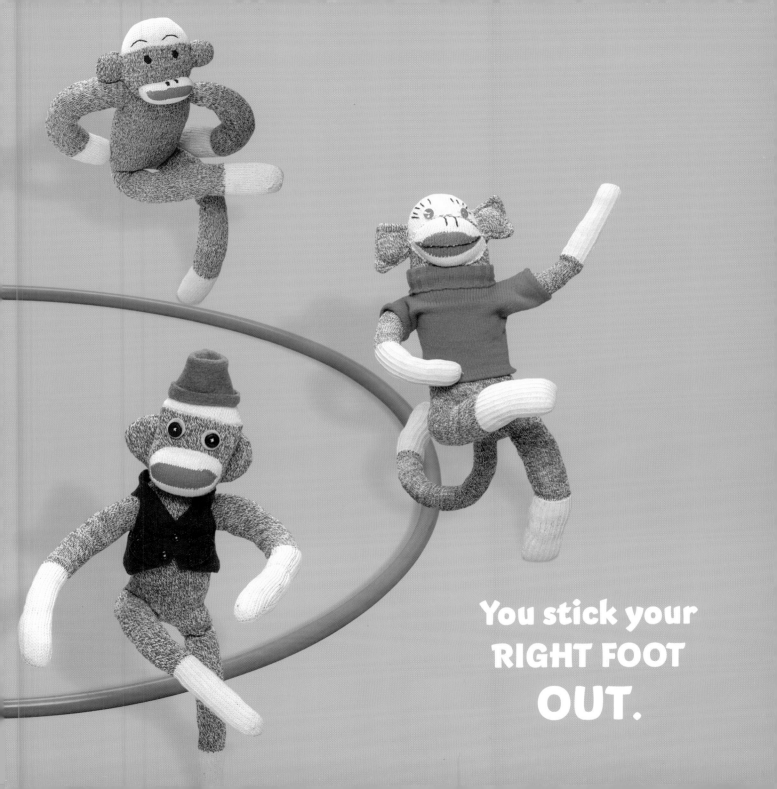

You stick your
**RIGHT FOOT
OUT.**

You do the MONKEY MONKEY
and you swing yourself around.

That's how
we dance and shout!

You stick your
LEFT FOOT
IN.

You stick your
**LEFT FOOT
OUT.**

You do the MONKEY MONKEY
and you swing yourself around.

That's how
we dance and shout!

You stick
your TAIL
IN.

You stick
your TAIL
OUT.

You do the MONKEY MONKEY
and you swing yourself around.

That's how
we dance and shout!

You stick your
ARMS and LEGS
IN.

You stick your
ARMS and LEGS
OUT.

You do the MONKEY MONKEY

and you swing yourself around.

That's how we dance and shout!